For Debbie, who has been in my corner
since I was ten—K.K.O.

To James Hanning—T. B.

STERLING and the distinctive Sterling logo
are registered trademarks of Sterling Publishing Co., Inc.

Library of Congress Cataloging-in-Publication Data

Orloff, Karen Kaufman.
Talk, Oscar, please! / by Karen Kaufman Orloff.   p. cm.
Summary: A boy imagines how much more fun he and his dog could have if only the dog would learn to talk.
 ISBN 978-1-4027-6563-6
 [1. Stories in rhyme. 2. Human-animal communication--Fiction. 3. Dogs--Fiction.] I. Title.
PZ8.3.O716Tal 2010   [E]--dc22

2008039930

Lot #:
2 4 6 8 10 9 7 5 3 1
11/10

Published by Sterling Publishing Co., Inc.
387 Park Avenue South, New York, NY 10016
Text © 2010 by Karen Kaufman Orloff
Illustrations © 2010 by Tim Bowers
Distributed in Canada by Sterling Publishing
c/o Canadian Manda Group, 165 Dufferin Street
Toronto, Ontario, Canada M6K 3H6
Distributed in the United Kingdom by GMC Distribution Services
Castle Place, 166 High Street, Lewes, East Sussex, England BN7 1XU
Distributed in Australia by Capricorn Link (Australia) Pty. Ltd.
P.O. Box 704, Windsor, NSW 2756, Australia

Sterling ISBN 978-1-4027-6563-6

For information about custom editions, special sales, premium and
corporate purchases, please contact Sterling Special Sales Department
at 800-805-5489 or specialsales@sterlingpublishing.com.

Talk, Oscar, PLEASE!

by Karen Kaufman Orloff   illustrated by Tim Bowers

STERLING

New York / London

Oscar, you yip
and, Oscar, you howl.

Oscar, you bark
and, Oscar, you growl!

Oscar, you whimper
and, Oscar, you wheeze.

Oh, boy, how I wish you could talk,
Oscar—please?

A dog that could talk would be totally cool!
I bet I could bring you along to my school.
You'll start out real simple, with your ABCs.
But first you should learn how to talk,
Oscar—please?

If you could talk, Oscar, you'd coach our new team.

When I kick the ball, you'll cheer and I'll scream!

You'll help me to score, with lots of "whoopee"s!

It sure would be great if you'd talk, Oscar—please?

On hikes, you could lead us
straight up a steep trail
and identify bugs as you
point with your tail.

You'll love the woods, Oscar—
so many big trees!
So open your mouth and just talk,
Oscar—please!

Won't it be great if Mom takes us to lunch?

You'll ask for some water, and I'll get fruit punch.

They'll serve you your favorite—bacon with cheese.

And we might get dessert, if you'd talk, Oscar—please?

If only you'd talk when we went out to play,
instead of just running, you'd have things to say.

You'll crack a few jokes, but I know you won't tease,
not like my big brother. So, talk, Oscar—please?

Maybe you'd like to be on a quiz show?

They'll ask you some questions, to see what you know.

You'll shout out the answers from "A" through the "Z"s.

You'll love being famous, so talk, Oscar—please!

Next time you feel sick and we go to the vet,

she'll say you're the cleverest dog that she's met,

because you'll explain that your problem is fleas.

I'll be awfully proud if you talk, Oscar—please?

And when I'm at Grandma's and you're all alone,
how fun would it be if we'd talk on the phone?

We'll laugh and tell stories. We'll just shoot the breeze.

We'll go on for hours. Just talk, Oscar—please?

When it's time for bed, it would be a surprise
if you'd come and sing me some dog lullabies
about collies and poodles, Great Danes, Pekingese . . .
You'd lull me to sleep if you'd sing, Oscar—please?

But, Oscar, sometimes when we're in my room playing,

I feel like I already know what you're saying.

Some people may laugh and think it's pretend . . .

. . . but I know it's true because you're my best friend.